PRI. LIB.

DATE DUE

Y0-AHQ-233

The Bus from Chicago

Many educators now believe that children as young as three years of age can learn to recognize and read words. Your young child can learn to do so with this EARLY-START Preschool Reader. It tells a story about an everyday situation familiar to all children. Only 49 different words are used to tell the story. These are repeated throughout the book, so that the child soon learns to recognize them and to understand their meaning.

The 49 words in this book are:

this	is	the	bus
from	Chicago	Mister	Gonzago
who	drives	driving	driven
grandma	with	boots	on
her	feet	getting	ready
so	she	can	meet
that	along	subway	under
ground	goes	going	a
loud	sound	to	take
station	Bill	and	his
mother	too	was	in
went	could	has	all
way			

Read this book through with your child a few times. Answer any questions that he asks about the words in the story. After two or three such readings, he will begin to show interest in reading the book by himself.

The Bus from Chicago

by Annie DeCaprio

illustrated by
Cal Sacks

WONDER BOOKS · NEW YORK
A Division of GROSSET & DUNLAP, Inc.

Copyright © 1965
Initial Teaching Alphabet Publications, Inc.
Publishers of Educational Materials in Pitman's i|t|a
20 East 46 Street, New York City, N. Y. 10017

All rights reserved. No part of this book
may be reproduced in any form without
the written permission of the publisher.

Printed in the United States of America
P-987654321

This popularly priced edition is a reprint in the traditional alphabet of a book originally published for schools in Pitman's Initial Teaching Alphabet.

Consultants:

Harold J. Tanyzer, Ph.D.
Hofstra University

Albert J. Mazurkiewicz, Ed.D.
Lehigh University

This is Mister Gonzago, who

drives the bus from Chicago.

This is the grandma
with boots on her feet,

getting ready so she can meet

the bus
that Mister Gonzago

is driving along from Chicago.

the bus that Mister Gonzago
is driving along from Chicago.

This is Bill and his mother, too,

going to meet the grandma who

was in the subway
under the ground

that went along with a loud, loud sound

to take the grandma with boots on her feet

to the bus station
so she could meet

the bus that Mister Gonzago

The Bus from Chicago

WASHINGTON CENTRAL SCHOOL